THORN OF CROWS

Laura Shenton

THORN OF CROWS

Laura Shenton

Iridescent Toad Publishing

Iridescent Toad Publishing.

First edition. ISBN 978-1-913779-14-6

Chapter One

The storm had passed, but its presence lingered like a half-forgotten nightmare, leaving the air heavy and restless with anticipation. The atmosphere was thick with contradictions: the earthy sweetness of rain-soaked soil mingled with the sharp, metallic tang that lightning always left in its wake, as though the sky itself had been wounded.

Sebastian, his feathers still damp from the downpour, maintained his vigil from his perch on the twisted limb of an ancient oak tree. The massive tree, gnarled and weathered by countless seasons, stood sentinel over the decaying grandeur of the estate below. From this carefully chosen vantage point, his keen eyes were fixed on a particular window in the manor's highest floor, where a pale figure moved like a restless spirit behind the gossamer veil of age-worn curtains. Elisa.

Her presence behind the filmy barrier was both ethereal and painfully real. She paced with the nervous energy of a caged creature, her shadowed form appearing and disappearing with each pass of the guttering candlelight that struggled against the darkness of her chamber. Even from his considerable distance, Sebastian could sense the crushing weight of whatever burden pressed upon her shoulders. It manifested in every aspect of her movement: the rigid set of her spine, the mechanical precision of her steps, the way her delicate hands repeatedly rose to press against her temples, as though she was physically trying to hold her thoughts from spilling out into the night air. There was something haunting about her fragility, yet it was coupled with an underlying tension that reminded Sebastian of a bowstring drawn too far, trembling on the very edge of either release or destruction.

Sebastian adjusted his position, his talons scraping against the rain-slicked bark as he sought better purchase on the ancient branch. The ritual had become familiar to him now: her endless pacing, the soft sighs that escaped her lips like captured prayers finally breaking free, the perpetual glances cast over her shoulder as though she was anticipating the arrival of something – or someone – that both terrified and fascinated her. He had maintained his watch for weeks, ever since that first fateful afternoon when he'd spotted her wandering through the untamed wilderness that had once been the manor's formal garden.

The memory of that day remained etched in his mind with perfect clarity: she had knelt among the wild roses that had long since broken free of their cultivated bounds, her fingers trailing over their velvety petals with an almost reverent touch. She had seemed oblivious to the thorns that caught and tore at her skin, drawing beads of dark blood that had fallen like rubies onto the hungry flowers below. The roses had appeared to drink in her essence, their red petals becoming somehow more vivid, more alive with each crimson drop they received.

That singular moment – the perfect crystallisation of vulnerability and quiet defiance – had forever ensnared her in

Sebastian's thoughts, binding her to him with invisible threads of fascination and concern.

The candlelight in Elisa's chamber flickered erratically, drawing Sebastian's full attention. Something felt different about tonight; there was a weight to the air that went beyond the mere aftermath of the storm. His feathers rustled with unease.

Behind him, the sound of wings cutting through the moisture-laden air announced another presence. Sebastian remained motionless, his focus unwavering. There was no need to turn; he knew who had joined him.

"She's not ours," Matthias' voice rumbled through the darkness, carrying the roughness of ancient stones being ground against each other. "You'd do well to remember that, before you lose yourself entirely to this obsession."

Sebastian maintained his silence, his gaze fixed unwaveringly on Elisa's window, where her slender silhouette had finally come to rest at the edge of her bed, though tension still radiated from her form like heat from a dying fire.

"She's human," Matthias pressed on, moving closer until his own clawed feet gripped the same rain-slicked branch. The older crow's presence was like a shadow given weight and substance. "And humans, they don't care for our kind. We exist only in their nightmares, their myths, their muttered curses against the dark."

"She doesn't curse us," Sebastian finally responded, his voice carrying the softness of falling snow yet imbued with unshakeable certainty. "She doesn't even see us. Not truly."

"That makes her no different from the rest of them. Perhaps even worse, for her blindness."

Sebastian's feathers bristled at the words, though he resisted the urge to engage in what would surely become a futile argument. Matthias carried the weight of years in every feather, his age evident in the steel-grey streaks that marked his wings and the sharp, weathered angles of his beak. He spoke with the bone-deep weariness of one who had witnessed too much of the world's darkness and had been carrying its burdens for far too long. Yet Sebastian couldn't – wouldn't – shake the certainty that Elisa was different. That she mattered in a way that defied his ability to express it in mere words.

The gentle whisper of disturbed leaves heralded another arrival, and Aurelia alighted beside them with the grace of a falling snowflake. She was the smallest of their trio, her feathers gleaming in a way that seemed to capture and reflect the very essence of moonlight.

"What draws his eye tonight?" she enquired, her tone carrying more genuine curiosity than the scepticism that coloured Matthias' words.

"She paces," Sebastian replied, his voice barely rising above the mournful whistle of the wind that wound its way through the estate. "She doesn't rest. She can't – or won't."

"She never does," Aurelia observed softly, a note of something like sympathy in her words.

Below their perch, the roses swayed in the

night breeze, their thorny vines writhing like dark veins across the cracked and broken stones that had once formed elegant garden paths. The garden's wild, untamed beauty seemed a perfect reflection of the woman who now haunted the manor's upper chambers. Sebastian's thoughts drifted to the rose he had claimed earlier that day, its petals as soft as silk and as red as fresh-spilled blood. It now rested in his private collection, hidden away in the hollow heart of a nearby tree, alongside other precious treasures he had gathered: a brass button that caught the light like a captured star, a triangular shard of broken glass that painted rainbow patterns on the bark in the morning sun, the preserved stem of another rose, its thorns still sharp enough to draw blood. They were tokens of something he couldn't quite name, pieces of a puzzle he was still trying to solve.

A sudden movement caught his eye, snapping his attention back to Elisa's window with the speed of a striking snake. The candlelight flickered once more, but this time Sebastian knew with soul-deep certainty that it wasn't the wind's doing.

The shadow that lurked in the corner of her

chamber appeared to shift and writhe, its edges curling and unfurling like smoke from a doused flame. Elisa remained oblivious to its movement, too consumed by her own internal struggles as she cradled her head in her hands, her shoulders trembling as though God himself had transferred the weight of his burden onto her slight frame.

"Do you see it?" Sebastian's voice cut through the night air like a blade, sharp with urgent concern.

"The shadow," said Matthias with a nervous shuffle in his feathers. "It's stronger tonight. More... purposeful."

"It's always there," Aurelia added, her usual lightness replaced by something darker, more knowing. "She just doesn't see it. Or perhaps she can't allow herself to see it."

Sebastian's talons dug deeper into the bark, carving fresh scars into the ancient wood. The shadow had been a constant companion to Elisa, always lurking at the edges of her world like a patient predator. It had been content to simply exist, darkening her days and haunting her nights from a distance. But tonight was different. Tonight, the shadow seemed more substantial, more defined in its purpose as it crept along the walls of her chamber, inching towards her with the deliberate patience of a hunter that had finally decided to claim its prey.

Within the confines of her room, Elisa shivered violently, as though someone had poured ice water down her spine. Her hand – trembling like an autumn leaf in a storm – reached for the small silver cross that hung from a delicate chain around her neck. She clutched it with the desperate strength of a drowning person grasping at a lifeline, as though the simple religious symbol could ward off the nameless dread that seemed to fill her chamber like smoke.

Sebastian's wings twitched with barely contained energy, every fibre of his being yearning to act. The urge to burst through the glass, to shatter the barrier between their worlds and drive back the encroaching darkness, was nearly overwhelming. But the cruel reality remained: he was just a crow, bound by the limitations of his form and the ancient rules that governed his kind.

"She's ours now," he declared quietly, the words carrying the weight of an oath, spoken more to the night itself than to his companions.

Matthias' response came in the form of a harsh caw, a sound that could have been either derisive laughter or a warning cry. "You're a fool if you think you can save her from what haunts her."

"I don't have to save her," Sebastian replied, his voice steady and certain. "I just have to help. That's all any of us can do."

As if in response to their exchange, the candlelight dimmed further, and the garden below seemed to darken in sympathy, the wild roses losing their ethereal glow as though the night itself was drinking in their colour. Sebastian spread his wings in preparation for flight, but Matthias' voice gave him pause.

"Don't let this destruction become your own," the old crow warned, his words heavy with the weight of hard-won wisdom.

Sebastian offered no response to the warning.

Instead, he launched himself from the branch, allowing the cool night air to catch his wings and carry him towards the manor's weathered walls. The glass of Elisa's window felt as cold as death as he landed on the narrow ledge. Inside, she had risen from her bed, moving with the cautious slowness of someone trying not to startle a dangerous animal. Her gaze was fixed on the corner where the shadow continued its sinuous dance, her breathing shallow and rapid like a frightened rabbit's.

Sebastian struck his beak against the glass, the sharp, decisive sound cutting through the heavy silence like a knife. Elisa whirled towards the sound, her eyes wide with a mixture of fear and wonder. She stared at him, her lips parting as though to speak, but whatever words she might have formed died unspoken in her throat.

Behind her, the shadow surged upward, its form stretching and distorting as it reached for her with tendrils of pure darkness.

Sebastian struck the glass again, harder this time, following the impact with a loud caw that seemed to shake the very air. The sound galvanised Elisa into action, driving her back several steps from the corner where the shadow writhed. Her fingers remained locked around the silver cross, knuckles white with the force of her grip.

The shadow appeared to hesitate, its movements becoming more languid, almost uncertain, as it drew back slightly from her retreating form.

For a long moment, the night held its breath. Then the candle gave one final sputter and died, plunging the chamber into complete darkness.

Sebastian's voice rose again, louder and more insistent, the sound echoing through the garden like a challenge to the darkness itself. Elisa stood frozen in place, her gaze locked on the window where he perched. For a brief, extraordinary moment, it seemed as though she truly saw him – not just as a bird, but as something more. Something other. The realisation of this seemed to soften her features, replacing fear with a different emotion entirely.

Yet the shadow remained, hovering at the

edges of the darkness like a promise – or a threat – of things yet to come.

Sebastian maintained his vigil on the window ledge until the first pale fingers of dawn began to creep over the horizon, painting the sky in delicate shades of pink and gold. Only then did he take wing, climbing the air currents back to the ancient oak where Matthias and Aurelia still waited, silent witnesses to the night's events.

"She's still alive," Aurelia observed softly, her words carrying both relief and apprehension.

"For now," Sebastian replied, his gaze already turning back towards the manor, where Elisa's window stood dark and silent in the growing light of day. "For now."

Chapter Two

The morning light crept across the estate with a peculiar quality that seemed to match the manor's melancholy spirit. It was a pale, anaemic sort of illumination that offered neither warmth nor comfort, the kind of light that served only to expose rather than to beautify. As it spilled over the manor's weathered face, it seemed to take particular delight in highlighting every imperfection: the cracks that mapped decades of neglect across the stone walls, the invasive vines that had positioned themselves like grasping fingers against the façade, their tendrils probing deeper into every fissure with each passing season.

Sebastian maintained his vigil from atop a particularly fearsome gargoyle that thrust out from the roof's edge, its grotesque features worn smooth by centuries of rain and wind. From this vantage point, he observed the first reluctant stirrings of human activity beginning to animate the grounds below.

The garden lay spread beneath him like a thorny tapestry, its wild roses and brambles glittering with countless beads of morning dew. These crystalline droplets clung to the thorns like tiny, precarious jewels, each one catching and fracturing the wan light into brief, cold sparkles. The thorns themselves seemed to wait with predatory patience, their sharp edges promising swift punishment to any who might venture too close without proper caution. They had long since claimed dominion over the garden's original paths and elegant stone benches, transforming what had once been an ordered paradise into a savage labyrinth where beauty and danger existed in perfect, terrible harmony. Among this threatening maze, the roses themselves bloomed with defiant splendour, their deep crimson petals maintaining their rich vibrancy even in the morning's ghostly illumination.

Sebastian's attention shifted regularly to Elisa's window, drawn there by an anxiety he couldn't quite suppress. She had not yet emerged into view, though the occasional flutter of movement behind the glass assured him she was awake and moving within her chamber. Sleep, he had observed, was something she seemed to regard as an unwelcome necessity, never allowing herself to remain in its embrace for any longer than absolutely required.

A shift in the morning breeze carried fragments of conversation to his keen ears. From the far side of the garden, Victor's voice cut through the peaceful stillness like a blade, his sharp tone carrying notes of both authority and distaste.

"She's pale enough to be a ghost herself," Victor declared, his words dripping with unconcealed disdain. "One might mistake her for one of the manor's spectral residents, if they were inclined to believe in such things."

Sebastian adjusted his position, elongating his neck to better observe the man as he made his way along one of the garden's less overgrown paths. Victor's boots struck the gravel with deliberate force, each step a small assertion of dominance over the ground itself. His clothing was impeccable, every piece clearly chosen and tailored to exhibit his wealth and position, yet there was something fundamentally off about his presence. A subtle wrongness emanated from him like a sour note in an otherwise perfect melody. It manifested in the mechanical precision of his movements, an impatience that seemed to radiate from his very being, and a coldness that suggested something far closer to cruelty than mere indifference.

"I don't see why she insists on remaining cooped up in that room like some sort of voluntary prisoner," Victor continued, his words clearly intended for his companion, a squat, solid man whose weathered face bore the same emotional range as the gargoyle upon which Sebastian perched. The man offered only a grunt of agreement, apparently understanding his role as an audience rather than a participant in the conversation.

Sebastian's feathers bristled with instinctive disapproval as he watched Victor pause beside one of the more magnificent rose bushes. With a casualness that bordered on contempt, the man extended his gloved hand

and plucked one of the blooms, paying no mind to the thorns that caught and pulled at the expensive fabric of his glove. He raised the flower to his face, inhaling its fragrance with exaggerated appreciation before discarding it with calculated carelessness, letting it fall to the gravel path where it would be crushed beneath the feet of subsequent wanderers.

The sight prompted a low warning caw from Sebastian's throat before he could suppress the impulse.

Victor's head snapped up at the sound, his eyes narrowing as they searched the roofline with sudden, sharp suspicion. Finding nothing to justify his unease, he shook his head as though dismissing an unwelcome thought and resumed his progress through the garden, his boots now deliberately crushing the fallen rose as he passed, leaving a trail of disturbed dust and broken petals in his wake.

Satisfied that he could now move unnoticed, with a powerful thrust of his wings, Sebastian launched himself from his gargoyle perch, allowing gravity to pull him into a controlled descent towards the garden below. The morning air rushed past him, cool and bracing, as he glided low over the rose maze, his keen eyes taking in every detail of the wild growth beneath him. He selected his landing site with careful precision, settling onto the weathered surface of a stone bench that had somehow maintained its dignity despite the garden's general descent into chaos.

The roses that surrounded him in this secluded corner of the garden had grown particularly wild and untamed, their petals displaying a shade of red so deep and rich it seemed almost supernatural, as though they had been nourished by something more vital than mere rainwater and soil. Sebastian hopped along the bench's edge, his sharp eyes methodically scanning the thorny branches for exactly the right specimen.

It had to be perfect – a precise balance between beauty's allure and danger's warning, a physical representation of the delicate line between desire and fear.

Near the bottom of one of the more robust bushes, he located exactly what he had hoped to find – a rose that had grown in sublime defiance of its circumstances, its stem curved in an elegant arc that spoke of resilience rather than weakness, unmarred despite its challenging position. With careful precision, he gripped the stem in his beak, mindful of the thorns that could easily pierce even his tough avian flesh as he worked to free it from its moorings.

This precious cargo was destined for his secret sanctuary, the hollow tree he had claimed as his private domain. The nook lay hidden within the massive roots of an ancient oak, where the earth maintained a perpetual dampness that seemed to preserve whatever was placed within it. There, among his carefully curated collection of treasures, he positioned the rose with deliberate care. Its petals seemed to capture what little light penetrated the hollow, transforming it into a small explosion of colour against the dark, age-smoothed wood of its new home.

The other objects in his collection, precious though they were, seemed somehow diminished in comparison to this new addition. The delicate gold chain of Victor's pocket watch caught what little light reached it, its coiled form reminiscent of a sleeping serpent waiting to strike. The timepiece itself lay cold and lifeless beside it, its once-pristine face now marred by a matrix of cracks. Sebastian had acquired it several days earlier, seizing an opportunity during one of Victor's infrequent absences from his study to pluck it from its resting place on the man's massive desk. Something about the object had called to him, though he couldn't quite articulate what quality had drawn his attention so forcefully.

It was, after all, merely a human contraption, a mechanical attempt to measure and control time itself. Yet for Elisa, time had become something more sinister – not a tool, but an adversary, each tick of the clock bringing her closer to something she seemed to dread with every fibre of her being.

***

As the day progressed, the garden gradually surrendered to silence, its human visitors retreating indoors to escape the increasingly bitter chill that had begun to permeate the afternoon air. Sebastian resumed his customary position near Elisa's window, observing her movements within the confines of her chamber. Her choice of dress reflected either simplicity or resignation – a pale, unadorned gown that seemed to emphasise rather than disguise her isolation from the ostentatious luxury that surrounded her.

Her hands betrayed her inner turmoil as she secured the ribbon at her waist, their slight but persistent trembling providing a stark contrast to the carefully composed expression she maintained. When she approached the window, Sebastian felt his heart quicken as her fingers traced patterns on the glass, leaving fleeting marks that faded like ghosts. For one hopeful moment, he thought she might actually open the window, might allow herself to feel the bracing kiss of the outside air and experience something real, something immediate, something other than the suffocating weight of her own thoughts.

But the moment passed unrealised.

Instead, she turned away, her attention drawn inexorably to the ornate mirror that dominated one corner of her room. The piece was a masterwork of craftsmanship, its frame adorned with intricately carved vines and flowers that seemed almost alive in certain lights. Sebastian had developed an intense hatred for the object, sensing something wrong in the way its glass seemed darker than it should be, more deeply reflective, as though it contained depths that no mirror should possess. And within those depths, the shadow waited and watched with hungry patience.

Even now, the spectral presence stirred within the mirror's surface, its movement like a ripple across the face of a pond on a windless night. Though Elisa showed no sign of conscious awareness of the entity's presence, her body betrayed her on a deeper level – her shoulders tensing, her posture becoming more rigid, as though preparing to defend against an attack she could sense but not see.

Sebastian voiced his frustration in a low, resonant croak, a sound meant to comfort himself as much as express his concern.

The shadow, he knew, could afford to be patient. It had been waiting for far longer than any mortal lifetime, and it could wait longer still.

***

Night descended upon the estate with unusual swiftness, as though the day had grown weary of maintaining even its weak illumination. Darkness wrapped around the manor like a funeral shroud, transforming the garden's vibrant roses into mere suggestions of colour in the growing gloom, their thorns now invisible but no less dangerous for their concealment.

Sebastian maintained his vigil as Elisa finally emerged from the sanctuary of her room, her footsteps barely audible against the ancient floorboards of the hallway. She moved with an ethereal quality that seemed more appropriate to a spirit than a living woman, her pale gown trailing behind her like mist as she made her way down the grand staircase.

Victor awaited her arrival in the manor's main parlour, his expression set in lines of obvious disapproval. A fire burned in the enormous hearth, its flames casting animated shadows across the room's elegant furnishings and creating an almost theatrical setting for what was to come.

"You look dreadful," Victor announced without preamble, his words seemingly designed to cut through any pretence of civility.

Elisa received this attack in silence, crossing the room with measured steps to position herself as far from him as the space would allow, maintaining her proud posture even as she kept her gaze carefully lowered.

Sebastian shifted his position on the window's outer ledge, his dark feathers rendering him nearly invisible against the night sky. From this vantage point, he could clearly perceive the tension that filled the room like a toxic gas, the unspoken resentment that seemed to crackle between them with almost physical force.

Victor's voice took on an even colder edge as he continued, "Your wedding is in a week. You might at least attempt to present yourself as a happy bride, rather than a condemned prisoner approaching the gallows."

Elisa's hands clenched into tight fists at her sides, but she maintained her silence, though Sebastian could almost feel the weight of the words she was forcing herself not to speak.

Sebastian's talons scored fresh marks in the wooden windowsill as he fought to contain his own rising frustration, a mirror of Elisa's carefully controlled anger. He could sense the spectral presence growing stronger, its hunger becoming more acute with each passing moment of tension.

Though he had no clear path to victory, no certain strategy for confronting an enemy he barely understood, Sebastian knew one thing with unshakeable certainty: he would not stand idle while the shadow claimed her. If there was to be a battle for Elisa's fate, he intended to ensure it would be one worth remembering.

Chapter Three

The endless succession of days melted one into another beneath a perpetual blanket of ash-coloured clouds, while bitter winds howled through the estate's ancient corridors like lost souls seeking refuge. With each passing hour, the spectre grew ever more audacious in its manifestations, no longer content to remain a mere glimpse at the edge of sight. Its ethereal form now wound itself around Elisa's figure with deliberate precision, its smoky tendrils coiling about her like a serpent preparing to strike, searching hungrily for any crack in her already fragile defences. Sebastian felt its malevolent presence as keenly as he felt the cruel bite of the thorns that surrounded his hollow in the ancient oak – a persistent, gnawing sensation that set his feathers on edge. The way the entity moved had become almost theatrical in its deliberateness, as though it derived some perverse pleasure from watching Elisa's once-vibrant spirit slowly dim, like a candle struggling against an inexorable wind.

From his various perches among the twisted branches of the estate's ancient trees, Sebastian maintained his vigilant watch over her increasingly concerning behaviour. On this particular afternoon, she had ventured into the neglected garden, though her movements betrayed none of the purpose or joy that had once characterised her daily constitutionals. Her steps were those of a sleepwalker, meandering and uncertain, her delicate hands hanging uselessly at her sides like broken wings. The relentless wind seemed to take particular delight in tormenting her hair, catching the pale silk ribbon that confined it and transforming it into a fraying banner of defeat. The hem of her once-pristine gown, now dulled by neglect, dragged carelessly through the muddy earth, collecting burrs and thorns from the garden's aggressive undergrowth as she wandered with increasing aimlessness along paths that had long since surrendered to nature's persistent advance.

Sebastian tracked her movements with unwavering attention, his powerful wings carrying him silently from one gnarled branch to another as he followed her meandering progress through the garden's decay. His dark feathers blended perfectly with the shadows cast by the threatening clouds above, making him nearly invisible to any who might chance to look upward. Elisa's wandering eventually brought her to the garden's centrepiece – a fountain that had once been the pride of the estate, its elaborate carvings and graceful lines now all but obscured beneath a suffocating blanket of creeping moss and determined ivy. The basin, which had once sparkled with crystal-clear water, now served only as a memorial to better days, its cracked surface acting as a repository for the garden's dead leaves and broken dreams.

She knelt before this monument to decay, her once-graceful movements now hesitant and uncertain. Her trembling fingers reached out to caress the brittle remains of what had once been a vibrant rose petal, its dried surface as fragile as her own tenuous grip on reality. Her lips moved in what might have been prayer or perhaps conversation with some unseen companion, but no sound emerged to disturb the garden's oppressive silence.

Sebastian cocked his head to one side, his keen eyes narrowing as his senses detected a disturbance in the air around them. It manifested as a subtle ripple, barely perceptible but growing stronger with each passing moment – a herald of the spectre's approaching presence that set every feather on his body on edge with anticipation and dread.

The sudden change in Elisa's demeanour was as jarring as a thunderclap in a silent room. She rose from her position by the fountain with such violence. Her movements, previously laden with lethargy, transformed into something approaching desperation – sharp, erratic gestures that spoke of a mind increasingly untethered from reality. She turned towards the rose bushes with an almost magnetic attraction, her hands stretching out before her like a blind woman seeking guidance in darkness. The thorns, cruel and unyielding, showed no mercy as they tore into the delicate flesh of her fingers, drawing crimson lines across her pale skin that bloomed like macabre flowers. Yet she seemed utterly oblivious to these self-inflicted wounds, as though her body had become merely a vessel for some greater, more consuming purpose.

Sebastian responded to her distress by descending to a lower vantage point, his wings carrying him to a branch that hung mere feet above her head. The aged wood creaked beneath his weight, a sound that seemed to echo the groaning of his concerned heart. He released a soft, deliberate caw – a sound carefully modulated to pierce through whatever fog had descended upon her consciousness, a gentle reminder that she was not alone in this growing darkness.

The effect of his call was immediate and profound. Elisa's entire body became a study in stillness, her bloodied hands suspended in the air above the roses like butterflies caught in amber. With agonising slowness, she rotated her head towards the source of the sound, her gaze travelling upward until it met his. The eyes that had once sparkled with vitality and intelligence now resembled nothing so much as twin pools of stagnant water – deep, dark, and utterly devoid of life.

The shadows beneath them spoke of countless sleepless nights spent battling unseen terrors, while something more insidious lurked in their depths, something that gnawed relentlessly at the foundations of her reason.

"Why are you here?" The words escaped her lips in a whisper so faint it might have been mistaken for the sighing of the wind through the garden's decay. The question hung in the air between them, laden with meanings that transcended its simple construction.

Sebastian responded to her query with a slight tilt of his head, his beak parting ever so slightly as though preparing to share secrets that his avian form rendered impossible to voice. The frustration of his enforced silence weighed heavily upon him, knowing that the truths she needed to hear were trapped within a body that could not give them voice.

She held his gaze for what seemed an eternity, her chest rising and falling in an irregular rhythm that betrayed her internal turmoil. Then, like a dreamer slowly surfacing from the depths of a nightmare, she gave her head a small shake and turned away, leaving the moment to dissolve like morning mist in the sun.

The garden lapsed once more into its customary state of desolation, disturbed only by the persistent rustle of wind-tormented leaves and the sharp cadence of Victor's voice carrying from the direction of the manor house. His words, though indistinct at this distance, carried the unmistakable edge of irritation as he addressed some unseen recipient – perhaps Harrison, the perpetually harried steward, or one of the few remaining maids who hadn't yet been driven away by the growing darkness that permeated the estate.

Sebastian took to the air once more, his powerful wings propelling him in wide circles above the garden as he attempted to track the spectre's elusive movements. The entity possessed an infuriating ability to slip through the shadows of the estate like water finding its way through the smallest of cracks, leaving only a lingering sense of unease in its wake. Earlier that day, he had observed it lurking in the corner of Elisa's chambers as she performed her morning toilette, its smoky tendrils reaching towards her reflection in the mirror with an almost loving caress.

Now it played its usual game of hide and seek, remaining just beyond the periphery of direct observation, biding its time with the patience of the truly immortal.

The flock had gathered in their usual meeting place – the massive oak tree that stood sentinel over the estate like an ancient guardian. Its branches, gnarled and twisted by centuries of growth, provided both shelter and concealment for their clandestine discussions. Aurelia, her feathers catching what little light managed to pierce the perpetual gloom, was the first to break the uncomfortable silence that had settled over their gathering.

"It's stronger than before," she observed, her melodious voice carrying undertones of barely suppressed anxiety. The slight ruffling of her feathers betrayed the depth of her concern, a concern that resonated through the entire flock.

"It's always been strong," Matthias countered, his gruff tone doing little to mask his own unease. His words carried the weight of bitter experience as he added, "We just didn't notice until now. Our own blindness has been our greatest weakness."

Sebastian alighted beside his companions, his wings folding against his back with practiced precision as he settled into position. His gaze remained fixed on the manor house, its weathered stones seeming to absorb what little light remained in the day. When he finally spoke, his words fell like stones into still water.

"It's not just stronger," he said, each word measured and deliberate. "It's hungry. And its appetite grows with each passing day."

His declaration was met with absolute silence, as though even the wind itself dared not challenge the truth of his words.

***

As darkness claimed its dominion over the estate, Sebastian resumed his self-appointed post outside Elisa's window. The single candle that illuminated her chamber fought a losing battle against the encroaching shadows, its flame dancing erratically as though responding to unseen drafts. The light it cast created an ever-shifting panorama of shadows that writhed across the walls like living things. Elisa sat curled in her favourite chair, her knees drawn up to her chest in a defensive posture that spoke volumes about her state of mind. Her arms wrapped around her legs with such force that her knuckles showed white against her skin, as though she feared that loosening her grip might cause her to come apart entirely.

The spectre had taken up its now-familiar position in the mirror, its form more substantially realised than Sebastian had ever witnessed before. The edges of its manifestation, usually soft and smoke-like, had acquired an almost crystalline sharpness that sent chills through his avian form. It observed Elisa with the focused attention of a predator studying its prey, its movements calculated and purposeful.

Sebastian's mounting concern drove him to tap his beak against the window glass with increasing urgency, the sound sharp and insistent in the night air. Elisa remained unmoved by his efforts, lost in whatever dark contemplation had claimed her attention.

Within the confines of the room, the spectre shifted its position with deliberate slowness. For the first time since Sebastian had begun his vigil, the entity's attention turned towards him, its focus falling upon him like a physical weight. The sensation of its regard was akin to being submerged in ice water – cold, invasive, and utterly without mercy.

Driven by desperate necessity, Sebastian released a caw that shattered the night's silence like breaking glass. The sudden sound finally penetrated Elisa's stupor, causing her to jerk upright in her chair, her wide eyes darting towards the window with the startled awareness of prey sensing danger.

For a brief moment, their gazes locked – human and avian united in their recognition of the peril that threatened. Then, as though following some unspoken cue, Elisa's attention shifted to the mirror, and the breath caught in her throat with an audible gasp of terror.

The spectre chose that moment to launch its attack, its form erupting from the mirror's surface like smoke from a suddenly stoked fire. Elisa's scream pierced the night air as she leapt from her chair and stumbled backwards, her movements frantic and uncoordinated. The candle's flame responded to the entity's presence with wild gyrations, threatening to extinguish itself and plunge the room into total darkness.

Sebastian reacted without conscious thought, hurling himself against the window glass with all the force his small body could muster. The impact sent shockwaves of pain through his form, but he persisted, striking again and again at the barrier that separated him from Elisa. His cries of desperation echoed through the night air, a counterpoint to the sounds of terror emanating from within the chamber.

Inside, Elisa had managed to regain her footing, her trembling hands clutching at the silver cross that hung from her neck. She thrust the sacred symbol before her like a shield, her voice breaking as she began to recite prayers in a desperate litany against the darkness that threatened to consume her.

The spectre recoiled from the combined assault of faith and Sebastian's determination, its sharply defined form dissolving once more into amorphous smoke as the candle's flame steadied, casting a warm glow that seemed to push back the shadows.

Exhaustion claimed Sebastian then, and he sagged against the window frame, his wings drooping with fatigue. Through the glass, he watched as Elisa collapsed to her knees, her hands still gripping the cross as tears carved glistening paths down her pale cheeks.

***

The hours until dawn stretched interminably, each moment weighted with the possibility of the spectre's return. Sebastian maintained his position at the window, his dark eyes fixed and alert despite his exhaustion. Not even the gentle coaxing of his fellow watchers could persuade him to abandon his post.

When the first tentative rays of morning light finally began to paint the eastern sky in delicate shades of pink and gold, Sebastian took wing at last. His flight path carried him directly to the hollow tree that served as a repository for his collection of significant objects – items gathered over time that held meaning beyond their physical presence.

To this carefully curated assemblage, he added a new treasure that morning – a single thorn, wickedly sharp and gleaming with malevolent purpose, plucked from the very bush that had drawn Elisa's blood during her garden wanderings.

The addition might have seemed insignificant to an outside observer, but Sebastian knew better. In this battle against encroaching darkness, every act of defiance, no matter how small, carried weight. The thorn would serve as both a reminder and a warning – a physical manifestation of his determination to protect Elisa from the shadows that sought to claim her, whatever the cost to himself might be.

Chapter Four

Dawn crept across the estate with painful reluctance, the sun struggling to disrupt the impenetrable fortress of clouds that had claimed dominion over the sky. The morning air hung heavy with moisture, carrying within its embrace the ancient perfume of rain-kissed stone and the delicate sweetness of dew-laden roses. From his position at the entrance of his hollow, Sebastian maintained his vigil over the grounds below, his obsidian eyes methodically scanning each shadow and corner of the vast estate. The memory of the previous night's encounter with the spectre weighed upon him like a physical presence, a dark companion that refused to release its hold on his thoughts.

The entity's attention – that moment when its consciousness had turned upon him with devastating focus – represented a fundamental shift in their strange relationship. For countless weeks, Sebastian had been the observer, carefully documenting the being's patterns and behaviours, studying its preferences and peculiarities with the dedication of a scholar. It had seemed content to exist as a thing of secrets and whispers, dwelling in the liminal spaces between reality and shadow. But last night, when its attention had fixed upon him with such terrible purpose, the dynamic had altered irrevocably. The spectre's regard had carried weight, intention, and most disturbingly, recognition.

His brooding contemplation was interrupted by the sudden displacement of air and the soft rustle of wings as Aurelia descended to join him. Her feathers caught what little light managed to pierce the gloom, creating an iridescent display that shifted between shades of midnight and twilight. She orientated herself beside him with careful precision, her keen gaze drawn inevitably to the collection of treasures that lay within his hollow – each item carefully chosen, each carrying its own significance.

"Your collection grows ever larger," she observed, her voice carrying the gentle timbre of raindrops on still water. "The thorn from yesterday, the rose you gathered last week, and even that curious bauble that belonged to the human woman."

Sebastian maintained his silence, his beak tightening almost imperceptibly as his attention shifted to Elisa's window. There, the subtle movement of heavy curtains revealed her presence, a ghost-like figure moving through the shadows of her chamber.

Aurelia edged closer, her movements deliberate and careful. "These tokens you gather... they hold no power against what haunts her. How can a thorn, no matter how sharp, hope to pierce the substance of a shadow? What protection can a withered rose offer against the encroaching dark?"

"They're more than just objects," Sebastian replied with deep conviction. "They're symbols, markers of significance. They carry meaning beyond their physical form."

"Perhaps they hold meaning for you," Aurelia conceded, her tone gentle but sceptical. "But does she perceive their significance? Does she even register their existence?"

Sebastian turned to face his companion then, his feathers rising slightly in a display of barely contained emotion. "Her awareness of them is irrelevant. My only concern is her survival. Nothing else matters."

Aurelia fell silent then, her expression softening as she recognised the intensity of feeling behind his words.

The ancient oak shuddered beneath the impact of Matthias' landing, his powerful wings dislodging a shower of leaves that spiralled down to join their brethren on the ground below. He had been observing their exchange from a distance, his razor-sharp vision missing nothing of Sebastian's increasingly obsessive behaviour.

"You're expending energy on a futile endeavour," he declared, his voice as heavy and oppressive as the leaden sky above them. "She's human, Sebastian. Their perception of reality is fundamentally different from ours. They stumble through life half-blind, barely aware of the true nature of the world around them."

"She's more aware than you realise," Sebastian countered, his attention never wavering from the manor house. "She senses the presence of things beyond her understanding. She feels the weight of watching eyes."

"What she feels is the product of her own fears and imaginings. Humans are masters of self-deception – they see phantoms in every shadow, hear whispers in every breeze."

Aurelia shifted uncomfortably on her perch, her wings rustling with nervous energy. "This is different, Matthias. You've witnessed it yourself. The darkness that surrounds her... it's not natural. It's not born of human fears."

Matthias released a contemptuous caw that echoed through the morning air. "I've walked this earth long enough to recognise darkness in all its forms. It comes like the tide, regular as moonrise, and like the tide, it eventually recedes. Humans lack the fortitude to withstand its touch – they crumble beneath the weight of their own imagined terrors."

"This is different," Sebastian interjected, his voice carrying an edge sharp enough to cut.

"This isn't some phantom born of her imagination. This is something ancient, something that has chosen her specifically. It stalks her with purpose, with intent."

Matthias studied him with the slow, deliberate focus of a judge weighing evidence. "And you believe yourself capable of preventing what's to come? You think your collection of trinkets and your constant surveillance will make any difference? Remember what you are, Sebastian. You're a crow, nothing more – bound by the limitations of your form."

Sebastian turned away from his elder's scrutiny, his feathers lying flat against his body in a display of contained emotion. "Perhaps being what I am is sufficient. Perhaps a crow is exactly what's needed."

***

The hours of daylight crawled past with excruciating slowness, each moment imbued with anticipation and dread. Elisa remained largely confined within the manor's walls, her presence marked only by occasional glimpses through various windows as she drifted from room to room like a restless spirit. From below, Victor's voice carried through the thick stone walls with remarkable clarity, his tone sharp with barely contained frustration as he issued commands to the dwindling household staff.

As the afternoon light began to soften, Sebastian maintained his vigilant patrol of the estate's perimeter, his wings carrying him in wide, careful circles as his keen eyes searched for any sign of the spectre's presence. The garden below lay in deceptive tranquillity, the roses swaying with hypnotic gentleness in the intermittent breeze. The peace felt artificial, like the stillness before a devastating storm.

Elisa had ventured out into the garden, her white gown standing out against the dark vegetation like a beacon in the gathering gloom. She moved with the hesitant grace of a sleepwalker, her attention fixed upon the roses as though they held some secret message meant only for her understanding. Sebastian had taken up position in the twisted embrace of an ancient willow when he detected something remarkable: a subtle distortion in the air, a place where light and shadow seemed to war with each other in defiance of natural law.

The spectre materialised at the far end of the garden path, its form possessing a solidity that Sebastian had never witnessed before. It moved with deliberate purpose, its edges rippling like smoke caught in a contrary wind as it advanced towards its intended prey.

Sebastian's warning cry split the air like thunder, shattering the garden's unnatural silence. Elisa's body went rigid, her head snapping up as her wide eyes darted frantically about, seeking the source of the disturbance.

Sebastian launched himself from his perch with explosive force, his powerful wings cleaving through the air as he hurtled towards the unfolding confrontation. Another warning cry tore from his throat, this one carrying all the urgency and terror that words could never fully express. Elisa spun towards the sound just as the spectre reached for her with grasping tendrils of darkness. She stumbled backwards in blind panic, her hands catching and tangling in the thorny embrace of the rose bushes behind her.

The spectre's advance faltered for a moment, its movements becoming uncertain, almost hesitant. Sebastian seized upon this moment of indecision, hurling himself towards the entity with reckless courage. His talons slashed through the space where its form writhed and twisted, challenging the very substance of shadow.

For one eternal moment, he felt something – a resistance that defied description, a sensation of cold so profound it seemed to freeze the very marrow of his bones. The spectre recoiled from his assault, its once-solid form dissolving into wispy tendrils of darkness that retreated into the deeper shadows of the garden.

Elisa crumpled to the ground like a puppet whose strings had been suddenly cut, her trembling hands still entangled in the rose vines. Fresh blood welled from multiple scratches across her palms, the crimson droplets stark and vivid against the pallor of her skin.

Sebastian landed a short distance away, his wings spread wide in an instinctive display of protective vigilance. She raised her head slowly, her eyes meeting his with an expression that mixed terror with dawning recognition.

"Why do you keep following me?" The words escaped her lips in a broken whisper, carrying equal measures of fear and desperate hope.

Sebastian met her gaze steadily, tilting his head in a gesture that conveyed more emotion than he could ever express through speech. How he longed to tell her that she wasn't alone in her battle against the darkness, that someone stood guard against the shadows that sought to claim her. But his form allowed him only a soft, gentle caw – a sound that nevertheless carried within it all the compassion and determination that filled his heart.

She held his gaze for what seemed an eternity before slowly gathering herself to stand. Though her movements remained unsteady, there was something different in her bearing now – a subtle straightening of her spine, an upwards tilt of her chin that spoke of awakening resistance. Without another word, she turned and made her way back towards the manor, her bloodied hands gathering the folds of her gown close about her.

***

As night descended upon the estate, the flock convened once more in their ancient oak. Aurelia perched in uncharacteristic silence, her usual luminous presence dimmed by the burden of recent events. Matthias occupied a higher branch, his feathers ruffled in agitation as he glared down at Sebastian with undisguised concern.

"Your actions today border on suicidal," Matthias declared, his voice harsh with worry disguised as anger.

"This isn't about my survival," Sebastian responded quietly, his gaze never leaving the manor house.

"Then enlighten us. What drives you to such reckless behaviour? Is it devotion to a human who barely acknowledges your existence? Or perhaps it's the futile desire to combat a force you can't possibly understand, let alone defeat?"

Sebastian's response came with unwavering certainty: "It's about standing against what's wrong, regardless of the cost."

Matthias' laugh carried no trace of humour, only bitter resignation. "You're behaving like a fool."

"That may be so," Sebastian admitted softly, his voice carrying the weight of absolute conviction. "But I won't abandon her to face this darkness alone."

A profound silence fell over the gathering then, each bird turning their gaze towards the manor where a single light burned with defiant brightness in an upper window – a lonely star in a sea of encroaching shadow.

Chapter Five

An otherworldly stillness had descended upon the estate, the kind of quiet that seemed to compress the very fabric of reality, as though the darkness itself had drawn closer, constricting the boundaries of the known world. The heavy clouds that had dominated the sky throughout the day had finally begun to fragment, revealing tantalising glimpses of the infinite expanse beyond. Through these celestial windows, stars pierced the darkness with diamond-bright clarity, while a delicate crescent moon painted the grounds below in subtle gradients of silver and shadow. Its ethereal light transformed the garden into a monochrome dreamscape, touching the rain-kissed roses and weathered stone paths with an almost supernatural luminescence.

Sebastian had taken up his customary

position on the worn ledge outside Elisa's window, his obsidian feathers melding seamlessly with the deeper shadows that clung to the manor's ancient walls. The atmosphere within her chamber was heavy with unspoken tension, thick enough that it seemed to press against the glass that separated them. Elisa sat perched on the edge of her bed, her posture suggesting both vigilance and exhaustion. Her hands, still bearing the evidence of her encounter with the rose thorns, were clasped tightly in her lap, her fingers working restlessly at the pale ribbon she had pulled from her hair earlier that evening.

The absence of her usual candle spoke volumes about her state of mind.

Sebastian observed her with careful attention, noting the increasing pallor of her skin and the deep shadows that had taken up residence beneath her eyes – physical manifestations of her ongoing battle with sleeplessness. Yet there was something different about her tonight, a subtle shift in her demeanour that caught his attention. A certain firmness had taken root in her expression, a nascent spark of determination that hadn't been present before. The tears that had become so familiar in recent weeks were notably absent, and Sebastian counted this small victory with cautious optimism.

The ornate mirror that dominated one corner of the room captured her diminished figure in its silvered surface, but tonight its glass remained remarkably placid, showing no signs of the spectral disturbances that had become commonplace. Sebastian wasn't fooled by this apparent respite; he knew the entity well enough by now to recognise its tactical retreats. It was merely biding its time, as it always did, waiting for the perfect moment to strike.

He adjusted his position slightly, his talons scraping against the weathered stone with a whisper-soft sound. Despite its faintness, the noise drew her attention immediately, her head turning towards the window with almost mechanical precision.

Their eyes met across the intervening space, and for a moment, time seemed to pause.

"You again," she said breathily, her voice carrying equal measures of wonder and uncertainty. She rose from her bed with deliberate slowness, each movement carefully measured as though she feared any sudden motion might cause him to take flight. "Why do you keep returning to this place?"

Sebastian maintained his position, meeting her questioning gaze with unwavering steadiness.

Elisa advanced towards the window with measured steps, her bare feet making no sound against the aged floorboards. She came to a halt just short of the glass, her hands hovering uncertainly near its surface as though contemplating opening it to the night air.

"There are those who say your kind brings ill fortune," she mused, her head tilting slightly as she studied him. "That death rides upon your wings like a dark passenger. Is that why you've chosen to haunt my window?"

Sebastian responded with a gentle croak, a sound carefully modulated to be neither ominous nor reassuring.

Her expression tightened slightly, her lips pressing into a thin line. Yet there was no fear in her scrutiny, only a profound curiosity, as though she sensed in him the possibility of answers to questions that had long plagued her. "Somehow," she said, speaking more to herself than to him, "I don't believe you're here with malicious intent."

With surprising decisiveness, she reached for the window's latch, releasing it with a soft click before pushing the heavy frame outward. The night air rushed into the room like an eager visitor, setting her nightgown aflutter with its cold caress. Sebastian remained motionless, even as her hand drew close enough that he could sense its warmth.

She hesitated, her hand suspended in the space between them, not quite daring to bridge the final distance. "Are you standing guard over me?"

The question hung suspended in the night air, fragile as a soap bubble and just as likely to burst at the slightest disturbance.

Sebastian responded by tilting his head slightly, allowing the weak moonlight to play across his feathers in a subtle display of iridescence.

A smile touched Elisa's lips then, though it was a weary thing, tinged with sadness and lacking the vitality that true joy should bring. "It seems you're the only one who's shown any real concern," she whispered, the words carrying a weight of loneliness that seemed to fill the room.

She withdrew her hand with reluctant finality, retreating from the window with measured steps. Sebastian tracked her movement as she approached the mirror, his attention sharpening as she positioned herself before its silvered surface. Her reflection stared back at her with hollow-eyed intensity, a perfect reproduction of her diminished form. For what seemed an eternity, she stood motionless before the glass, her fingers absently tracing the contours of the silver cross that hung at her throat – a gesture that seemed both protective and unconscious.

"I can sense its presence," she confided, her voice barely more substantial than a breath. "Even in moments of solitude, when the house lies silent and still. Its gaze never wavers, never ceases its vigil."

The mirror's surface remained undisturbed, its depths showing nothing but the expected reflection. The shadows maintained their proper places, giving no hint of supernatural disturbance. Yet Sebastian recognised the truth in her words.

***

Time crawled forward with glacial slowness, the profound silence broken only by the occasional protestation of ancient timbers as the manor settled deeper into its foundations. Elisa eventually surrendered to exhaustion, though not to true rest, curling onto her side atop the bed with her knees drawn protectively to her chest. Her breathing fell into an irregular rhythm, suggesting a state of half-consciousness rather than genuine slumber.

Sebastian maintained his watch until her movements stilled entirely before spreading his wings to take flight. The night air caught him in its embrace as he soared above the sleeping garden, his keen vision penetrating the darkness to study the paths below. The roses that lined the walkways had been transformed by darkness into abstract sculptures, their thorns concealed within the velvet shadows.

His flight path carried him towards his hollow, that sacred repository of carefully collected treasures. As he approached, the pocket watch's golden chain caught and reflected the moon's faint illumination, creating a subtle constellation against the weathered wood of his sanctuary. His gaze was drawn to the rose he had gathered days earlier, its once-vibrant petals now transformed by time into delicate fragments of their former glory.

Instead of immediately retreating, with careful precision, he selected another thorn from the nearby rose bushes, taking great care to avoid its razor-sharp edges. Though it was modest in size, barely matching the length of his beak, it possessed a cold and deadly beauty that seemed to capture the essence of the garden's darker nature. He transported it with reverence to his hollow, placing it with deliberate care alongside the watch and the other tokens he had accumulated over time.

These objects were more than mere trinkets, more than simple curiosities collected by a creature drawn to bright things. They were symbols, yes, but they also represented potential – tools with a true purpose yet to be revealed. Though he couldn't articulate how or why, Sebastian felt with unshakeable certainty that these items held significance beyond their physical form, that they already played a role in the unfolding drama, even if that role remained unclear.

***

When Sebastian returned to his vigil at the manor, the night had deepened considerably. The air had taken on a sharper edge, and the wind had transformed from a gentle whisper to a howling presence that tore through the ancient trees with savage intent.

He reclaimed his position on the windowsill, his dark eyes conducting a thorough survey of the chamber within. Elisa was awake, though she hadn't altered her position on the bed. Her eyes were fixed upon the ceiling, studying its worn surface as though the answers to all of life's mysteries might be found in its aged plaster.

The shadows in the room's corners began to shift with subtle purpose.

Sebastian's feathers bristled in immediate response to the threat, his body tensing as he observed the spectre's materialisation. It manifested with uncharacteristic deliberation, its form barely distinguishable as it wove through the darkness like smoke through water. Its movements were calculated and precise as it advanced towards the bed with predatory intent.

Sebastian shattered the oppressive silence with a sharp, commanding caw that seemed to physically slice through the quiet. Elisa bolted upright, her eyes wide with recognition as they sought out his form at the window.

"It's here, isn't it?" she whispered, her voice trembling with a mixture of fear and terrible certainty.

She didn't waste precious moments waiting for confirmation she knew wouldn't come. Instead, she lunged for the candle that sat on her bedside table, her hands shaking visibly as she struggled with the match. After what seemed like an agonising while, the wick caught the flame, spreading a weak but steady illumination throughout the space.

The spectre recoiled from the light's advance, its form dissolving into wispy tendrils as it retreated to the room's darker recesses.

Elisa clutched the candle before her like a shield against the darkness, her breathing gradually steadying as the immediate threat receded. Her gaze found Sebastian once more, recognition and gratitude mingling in her expression.

"Thank you," she murmured, the simple words laden with profound appreciation.

Sebastian maintained his position at the window, his unwavering gaze fixed upon her as the candlelight worked its subtle magic, slowly calming her trembling hands and racing heart.

***

As the first hints of dawn began to paint the eastern sky in subtle shades of pearl and rose, the spectre withdrew completely, retreating to whatever shadowy realm it called home during daylight hours. Elisa finally surrendered to genuine sleep, her head coming to rest against the pillow while the candle continued its faithful vigil, its flame burning low but steady.

Sebastian remained steadfast at his post, his dark silhouette etched against the lightening sky like an ancient sentinel. His form, though small against the vastness of the manor's façade, carried with it an air of indomitable purpose – a guardian set against powers far greater than himself, yet unwavering in his determination to stand between innocence and the darkness that sought to claim it.

Chapter Six

The day began with a grim and pervasive stillness, settling like a burial shroud over the sleeping earth and pressing heavily on the chests of every living creature. Each breath drawn seemed muted and hesitant, as though the very air itself possessed enough wisdom to hesitate before disturbing the quiet that had descended upon the manor grounds with inexorable purpose.

From his strategic perch in the ancient oak's twisted and gnarled branches, positioned to afford him the clearest view of the unfolding tragedy, Sebastian watched with growing unease as the manor house gradually awakened to face the looming day, its usual robust symphony of movement and morning sound subdued to little more than whispers against the hollow silence. The air carried an inexplicable yet undeniable tension that, while impossible to trace to any single source, pressed against every surface with the suffocating burden of approaching calamity.

Elisa's wedding loomed before them all like a threatening storm gathering force on the distant horizon, its dark promise casting long shadows over every preparation and quiet conversation. The wedding preparations, already dampened by her increasingly obvious reluctance and growing despair, had taken on the aspect of some elaborate theatrical performance, with each participant moving through their assigned role with mechanical precision and carefully averted eyes that spoke volumes about their silent discomfort. Servants scurried between the imposing manor house and the small chapel nestled at the edge of the estate like worried mice seeking shelter from an approaching predator, their arms laden with pristine white linens that seemed to glow with an almost surreal radiance against the dreary morning light and delicate glass lanterns that caught and scattered what little sunshine managed to pierce the dense canopy of clouds overhead. The chapel's bell tower, its ancient stone face marked by a prominent crack that ran like a deep battle scar from base to peak, leaned slightly to one side as though attempting to distance itself from the proceedings about to unfold beneath its weathered gaze, standing as a silent but judgmental witness to the human drama playing out in its shadow.

In the meticulously tidied garden, where every blade of grass seemed to have been measured and cut to precise specifications, Victor moved between the carefully tended flower beds with the detached air of a man surveying his dominion. His expensive boots, polished to such a brilliant shine that they reflected the clouded sky like dark mirrors, pressed against the carefully laid gravel beneath them with each precise step, the sound crisp and measured in the morning quiet. His voice, cultured and distant as a winter moon, drifted through the stillness as he addressed a young maid who struggled to arrange an elaborate bouquet of roses, her fingers trembling slightly under his impassive observation.

"That will need to be done again," he stated with the cool detachment of one commenting on the weather, his gloved hands gesturing dismissively at her efforts. "The arrangement lacks the proper symmetry. One expects a certain standard of excellence on such an occasion. Perhaps someone with more experience should be assigned to the task." His words fell like autumn frost, neither heated nor particularly cruel, but chilling nonetheless in their complete lack of warmth.

Sebastian tilted his head to observe the scene more closely from his elevated position, his feathers rising in quiet agitation as he watched the rose's natural thorns catch against Victor's expensive gloves, their ancient defences holding firm against his casual handling. For a brief moment, he considered how satisfying it might be to swoop down from his secure perch, if only to disrupt the man's perpetual composure. But no – he forced the impulse aside with considerable effort. His sacred duty lay with protecting Elisa from the darkness that gathered around her, not with disturbing her betrothed's carefully maintained veneer of sophistication.

Within the manor's oppressive walls, which seemed to lean inward with silent judgment like disapproving observers, Elisa drifted through the grand halls like a spirit already departed from the mortal realm, existing simultaneously in this world and some darker place beyond human understanding. Her wedding gown, an undeniable masterpiece of white silk and impossibly delicate lace that should have been a triumphant celebration of beauty and craftsmanship, hung from her increasingly diminished frame like a costume borrowed from another's wardrobe, its generous proportions suggesting it had been designed for someone else entirely –someone stronger, someone who might approach the altar with joy and anticipation rather than the quiet resignation that seemed to radiate from her very being. Her hair, left to fall in soft waves that caught what little light filtered through the towering windows, seemed to possess the ability to absorb the weak sunlight and transform it into a halo of amber and gold around her pale face, creating an ethereal effect that only served to emphasise her increasingly otherworldly appearance and growing detachment from the physical realm.

And always, always, the melancholy spectre

maintained its careful vigil over her every movement.

It lingered with patient purpose in the deepest shadows of the hallway, its form simultaneously substantial and insubstantial, like smoke given conscious purpose by some force beyond mortal comprehension. Its fluid movements perfectly mirrored her own with a precision that spoke of long companionship, each hesitant step she took drawing it incrementally closer to her vulnerable form, its edges perpetually shifting between definition and dissolution like a dream caught between sleeping and waking, curling and uncurling like tendrils of mist testing the boundaries of what little light remained in her world.

Sebastian tracked her painfully slow progress from window to window with growing concern, his powerful wings twitching with the desperate need to take immediate action against the forces gathering around her. From his various carefully chosen vantage points along the manor's façade, he could see every nuance of her mounting distress with perfect clarity – the way her increasingly delicate hand trailed along the wall for desperately needed support, her trembling fingers pressing against the expensive wallpaper as though she might dissolve entirely without its steady presence beneath her touch, the slight but unmistakable tremor in her uncertain steps that spoke eloquently of exhaustion both physical and spiritual, as though her very soul had grown weary of maintaining its connection to her mortal form.

When at last she reached the small parlour where Victor awaited her presence with characteristic reserve, Sebastian alighted with silent grace on the narrow stone ledge outside the leaded glass window. Though the thick, ancient glass muffled their exchange of words, he could discern enough of their conversation to understand the underlying current of resignation and quiet submission that informed their every interaction.

"You look pale," Victor observed with clinical detachment, his tone carrying all the warmth of a midwinter morning. "One might hope for more enthusiasm on such an occasion." The words were neither cruel nor kind, merely stating what he perceived as an unfortunate fact.

"I'm fine," Elisa responded with visible effort, though her voice wavered like a candle flame caught in a draft, entirely failing to convince anyone who might be listening.

Victor crossed the space between them with measured steps that seemed carefully calculated to maintain proper social distance, his gloved hand rising to gesture vaguely in her direction as though pointing out a painting that failed to meet his exacting standards.

"You'll do, I suppose," he pronounced after a moment of critical assessment, stepping back to examine her as a curator might appraise a new acquisition for his carefully acquired collection. "But remember this well: after today, certain standards must be maintained. Your habit of wandering the grounds at night, your frequent absences from social gatherings – these eccentricities reflect poorly on the position we must maintain in society. I trust you understand the necessity of conducting yourself with appropriate dignity once we are married."

Sebastian's talons scraped lightly against the weathered window ledge in quiet frustration, leaving shallow marks in the ancient stone that would endure long after this day had passed into distant memory. The sound, though far too faint for human ears to detect, provided him with a small measure of satisfaction as he contemplated the vast difference between Victor's carefully maintained exterior and the cold emptiness that lay beneath.

By mid-afternoon, the ancient chapel had undergone a transformation that struck Sebastian as both beautiful and deeply unsettling. Its weathered stone walls, each block worn to a silken smoothness by centuries of punishing winds and relentless rains, now disappeared beneath elaborate cascades of pale silk that had been arranged with painstaking precision. These ethereal draperies stirred and swayed with each whisper of breeze that found its way into the sacred space, their movement reminiscent of restless spirits attempting to break free from their earthly tethers. The overwhelming fragrance of roses saturated every corner and crevice of the chapel, their sweetness taking on an almost narcotic quality in the enclosed air, growing heavier and more cloying with each passing moment until it seemed to settle like a suffocating blanket over the entire proceedings.

The spectre had followed them to this hallowed ground, just as Sebastian had known it would. There was an inevitability to its presence that made his feathers bristle with barely contained anger.

From his elevated vantage point, Sebastian observed its malevolent presence as it lurked within the shadowy confines of the bell tower, its formless shape growing steadily more distinct and substantial as the afternoon light began its slow descent towards evening. The entity seemed to pulse and throb in perfect synchronisation with Elisa's mounting despair, drawing sustenance from her growing hopelessness like a parasite feeding on its unwilling host, waiting with an infinite and terrible patience for the ceremony to begin in earnest.

The flock had gathered in strategic positions throughout the massive oak tree that had stood as an ancient sentinel over the chapel for untold centuries, its gnarled branches providing them with an unobstructed view of the unfolding tragedy below. Matthias, who had always served as the voice of caution and restraint among them, maintained his characteristically grim countenance, his usually sleek feathers ruffled in visible agitation against the strengthening wind that swept across the chapel grounds.

"It's not our place to interfere in matters such as these," he declared, each word laden with resignation and ancient wisdom. "Some fates, no matter how tragic they may appear to our eyes, must be allowed to play out as destiny intends. We are witnesses, not arbiters."

"It is precisely our place to intervene," Sebastian countered with quiet intensity, his penetrating gaze never wavering from the bell tower where darkness gathered like the prelude to a tempest. "If not ours, then whose? Who else stands between her and what approaches?"

"You truly believe you possess the power to prevent what's coming?" Matthias scoffed, though genuine concern threaded through his derision like silver through stone. "Even with all your strength, you can barely slow its advance, let alone halt it completely. Some forces lie beyond our ability to counter."

Sebastian maintained his resolute silence, unable to offer a convincing rebuttal to this uncomfortable truth that lay between them like a shadow.

Aurelia, whose wisdom often served as a bridge between their conflicting viewpoints, fluttered closer to them both, her movements betraying an uncharacteristic uncertainty that sent a chill through Sebastian's heart. "What if Matthias speaks with the voice of wisdom in this matter?" she ventured, her voice barely more substantial than a whisper on the strengthening wind. "What if this situation truly lies beyond our power to influence, beyond even our considerable abilities to shape?"

Sebastian turned to face her then, his dark eyes sharp with unwavering purpose and barely contained fury that seemed to radiate from his very being. "If we stand idle now, if we choose the path of inaction, she is irretrievably lost to us all," he declared with quiet intensity that seemed to make the very air around them vibrate with conviction. "The spectre will claim her entirely, body and soul, and Victor will inter whatever remains of her broken spirit in this place forever, binding her to these stones until time itself crumbles to dust. I cannot – will not – allow such a fate to befall her while I draw breath."

When at last the dreaded ceremony commenced, the chapel's sacred space filled with the subdued murmurs of the assembled guests, though they were surprisingly few in number for an event of such supposed significance. Most of those present were distant relations of Victor's, their expressions uniformly crafted into bland masks of polite disinterest, as though they were attending a slightly tedious business meeting rather than bearing witness to the binding of two souls. The air hung heavy with forced solemnity and unacknowledged tension that seemed to press down upon all present like a physical weight.

Elisa stood before the ancient altar like a sacrificial offering awaiting the ceremonial blade, her hands visibly trembling as they clutched the carefully arranged bouquet of blood-red roses. Against the backdrop of dark, ancient stone that seemed to absorb what little light remained in the chapel, she appeared almost translucent, as though she might fade from existence entirely at any moment, leaving nothing behind but a memory of grief. Her expression remained carefully, deliberately blank, a mask crafted from years of survival, though her eyes held shadows deeper than any natural darkness Sebastian had ever witnessed.

Victor loomed beside her, his presence seeming to press her further into the ground with each passing moment, as though he sought to bury her beneath the very stones of the chapel floor. His carefully controlled expression did little to mask the possessive gleam in his eyes, a hunger that Sebastian had seen all too often in predators of both the natural and supernatural worlds.

The spectre, sensing its moment of triumph approaching with inexorable certainty, began to move with terrible purpose through the gathered shadows.

Sebastian detected its motion first, his senses attuned to the slightest disturbance in the natural order. He watched with mounting dread as its amorphous form shifted position in the deeper shadows near the altar, flowing like black water between the ancient stones. The creature's outline grew sharper, more defined with each passing second, its edges no longer fluid but crystallising into something with clear intent and deadly purpose. The darkness it emanated seemed to absorb what little remaining light filtered through the chapel's stained glass windows, creating a void that threatened to swallow everything in its path.

Elisa's breathing quickened perceptibly, her chest rising and falling in sharp, irregular movements beneath the confining bodice of her ivory gown. Her gaze darted towards the ornate mirror that hung behind the altar, its gilded frame catching and reflecting the flickering light of nearby candles, and her eyes locked onto the spectre's reflection with horrified recognition that spoke of long nights filled with terror. Her grip on the bouquet tightened convulsively, driving the imperfectly trimmed thorns deep into her flesh with enough force to draw blood. Bright crimson droplets welled between her trembling fingers, falling like tears to stain her pristine pale skin with stark crimson blooms that spread like watercolours on silk.

Sebastian issued a sharp, piercing cry from his position in the ancient rafters, his voice echoing through the chapel's vaulted ceiling like a warning bell tolling in the night. The assembled guests turned their faces upward in startled confusion, their carefully maintained expressions of polite boredom cracking to reveal genuine alarm, but he paid them no mind. His warning was intended for other ears entirely, for those who could understand the true meaning behind his call.

The spectre, perhaps sensing that its moment of advantage was slipping away like sand through an hourglass, launched itself forward with terrible purpose that seemed to make the very air grow thick with malevolent intent.

Chaos erupted within the sacred space like a geyser breaking through stone, shattering the careful veneer of civilisation that had been maintained up until that moment.

Elisa's scream broke the ceremonial silence like a boulder through glass, her carefully arranged bouquet falling from bloodied fingers to scatter roses across the stone floor like drops of blood on freshly fallen snow. She stumbled backwards in blind panic, her heel catching on the trailing edge of her elaborate gown. Victor reached for her with possessive hands that seemed more like claws in the failing light, his expression contorting with a mixture of rage and embarrassment that transformed his handsome features into something grotesque, but the spectre moved with speed that defied all natural laws.

Its dark form enveloped her like a funeral shroud, writhing tendrils of shadow wrapping around her arms and throat with terrible purpose that spoke of long-planned malice. The darkness seemed to pulse with a life of its own, each beat matching the rapid rhythm of Elisa's terrified heart as it sought to claim her completely.

Sebastian launched himself from his perch among the ancient rafters without hesitation, his wings cutting through the air with deadly precision as he aimed his attack at the very heart of the shadow entity. His talons struck home with a force that would have felled any natural creature, meeting a resistance that felt like plunging into waters beneath winter ice, sending waves of bone-deep cold through his entire being. The spectre recoiled from the unexpected assault, its form temporarily dissolving into wispy strands of darkness that writhed like dying snakes before reforming near the altar, gathering its strength for another attack that promised even greater violence.

The assembled guests abandoned any pretence of dignity or social graces, their cries of terror and confusion echoing off the stone walls as they fought their way towards the chapel doors, pushing and shoving in their desperate haste to escape whatever darkness had invaded their carefully ordered world. Victor remained rooted in place as though turned to stone, his face draining of all colour as he stared at the manifesting spectre with the first genuine expression of fear Sebastian had ever witnessed on his carefully controlled features.

Elisa collapsed to her knees on the hard stone floor, her bloodied hands clutching desperately at the silver cross suspended from her neck as though it represented her last hope of salvation. Her prayers emerged as broken whispers, desperate and disjointed, but they carried an unexpected power that seemed to force the spectre back several paces, its form wavering like smoke in a strong wind. Each word that fell from her lips seemed to gather strength from some deep well of faith that even she had not known she possessed.

Sebastian landed beside her with graceful precision, his feathers ruffled but unbroken by his encounter with the entity, his presence steady and unwavering in the face of the paranormal chaos that threatened to overwhelm them all. He voiced a soft, reassuring call, the sound carrying meanings that transcended the limitations of human language, speaking directly to something deep within Elisa's soul that recognised truth when it was presented.

She turned to look at him then, her tear-stained face transformed by a flash of recognition that suggested she truly saw him for what he was for the first time – not merely a bird, but something far more ancient and powerful, a guardian whose kind had watched over humanity since the first prayers were whispered into the darkness.

When the last echoes of chaos finally faded from the chapel's vaulted ceiling like a distant rumble, Elisa rose slowly to her feet with a grace that spoke of newfound strength. Her wedding gown was torn and stained with blood from her wounded hands, the pristine white fabric now bearing witness to the battle that had been fought, but her eyes burned with a fierce inner light that transformed her entire countenance. The weak, frightened girl who had entered the chapel what felt like ages ago had been burned away in the crucible of confrontation, leaving something stronger and more resolute in her place.

She turned to face Victor, who stared at her with an expression caught between murderous rage and stunned disbelief, as though he was seeing her truly for the first time and could not reconcile this new version with the docile creature he had sought to possess.

"This is over," she declared, her voice carrying a strength and certainty that belied the tremors still visible in her hands, each word ringing with truth against the ancient stones. "Whatever power you thought you held over me dies here, today, in this place where you sought to imprison my spirit."

Victor took a menacing step towards her, his familiar mask of control cracking completely to reveal the true darkness that had always lurked beneath the surface of his carefully maintained façade, but she held her ground. She turned with deliberate grace and walked towards the chapel doors, her steps measured and unwavering despite the lingering atmosphere of discomfort, each footfall striking the stone floor like a declaration of independence.

Sebastian took wing one final time, following her path through the broken silence as the spectre's form flickered and faded like a candle being extinguished by a sudden breath, leaving only the faintest trace of shadow to mark its exit from the scene. In its wake, the chapel seemed to exhale, as though released from a long-held breath that had threatened to suffocate all within its walls, while moonlight streamed through the windows with renewed brightness, illuminating the scattered rose petals that marked Elisa's path to freedom like blazing stars against the ancient stone floor.

Chapter Seven

The air outside the chapel hung thick and cold, an almost tangible presence that wrapped around Elisa like a shroud as she stepped into the deepening night. The bitter wind pulled insistently at her torn wedding gown, the once-pristine fabric now stained and ragged, while carrying with it the overwhelming sweetness of crushed roses mingled with the acrid, metallic scent of fear that lingered in the wake of the spectre's violent manifestation. Above her, the chapel's ancient bell hung motionless in its tower, its rusted form as useless against the supernatural horrors that had erupted within the sacred space as it would be against the coming dawn.

Sebastian wheeled overhead in wide, watchful circles, his obsidian wings cutting clean lines through the pale moonlight that struggled to pierce the gathering clouds. Below his vigilant patrol, Elisa's steps grew increasingly uncertain as she made her way along the overgrown path that led back towards the looming shadow of the manor house. Her trembling fingers remained locked around the silver cross suspended from her neck, its surface smeared with blood from where the roses' thorns had torn her flesh. Her breathing came in shallow, irregular gasps that barely seemed to provide enough air to keep her conscious.

"Where can she possibly go?" Aurelia's voice drifted up from the ancient oak where the remainder of the flock had gathered to witness the unfolding drama, her usual confidence replaced by genuine concern.

Sebastian swooped lower, his keen gaze never leaving Elisa's stumbling form. "Anywhere," he replied with fierce conviction, "anywhere but here, where shadows and cruelty have equal claim to her soul."

"You know she lacks the strength to fight it," Matthias countered in a low growl, his tone heavy with grim certainty. "The shadow will pursue her wherever she flees. It always does. Such is its nature."

Sebastian alighted near the garden's crumbling boundary, his sharp talons finding purchase in the weathered stone of a fallen statue, its features worn smooth by time and neglect. From this vantage point, he observed Elisa as she stumbled into the formal garden, her movements growing more laboured with each step, as though she carried within her very bones the lingering cold of the spectre's ethereal touch.

"She need not face this battle alone," Sebastian declared, his voice carrying an unwavering certainty that seemed to challenge the very darkness itself.

Elisa collapsed to her knees among the carefully tended roses, their dark blooms swaying in an unseen current that seemed to have little to do with the natural movement of air. Her hands, pale and trembling, plunged into the rich soil with desperate purpose, her perfectly manicured nails becoming dirty as she clawed at the damp earth like one possessed. Though no tears fell from her wide eyes, her breathing had devolved into harsh, wounded sounds that seemed torn from the depths of her very being.

The spectre's presence pressed against the boundaries of perception.

Sebastian could feel its malevolent weight bearing down upon the night, an unnatural cold that seemed to draw the very warmth from living flesh. The rest of the flock sensed it too – Matthias maintained his position high in the oak's protective branches, his feathers puffed out against more than mere physical chill, while Aurelia shifted restlessly from perch to perch, unable to find comfort in any single position.

"It watches her with such intensity," Aurelia observed in a tremulous whisper, her bright eyes darting repeatedly towards the darkened garden. "What drives such focused malevolence? What could it possibly want from her?"

"Everything she is," Matthias responded with characteristic grimness. "Everything she was. Everything she might become."

Sebastian made his way closer to Elisa's huddled form, his movements utterly silent as he crossed the disturbed earth. She remained oblivious to his approach at first, her entire being focused on the compulsive act of digging, as though she might unearth some salvation in the garden's dark soil. It wasn't until her searching fingers wrapped around the thorny stem of a buried rose that she finally stilled, her head lifting slowly to meet his unwavering gaze.

"You've returned again," she whispered, her voice roughened by screams and terror. "You're always here when darkness falls."

Sebastian cocked his head to one side, his obsidian eyes catching and reflecting the wan moonlight. He offered a soft, low caw, pitching the sound to convey reassurance rather than alarm.

Elisa regarded him with an intensity that suggested she was trying to pierce the veil between their worlds, to understand something that hovered just beyond her grasp. After a long moment, she shifted her attention to the rose she had unearthed, its petals so dark they seemed to absorb what little light reached them. The stem bristled with cruel thorns that continued to draw blood from her already wounded fingers, the crimson drops falling to stain the midnight blooms with even deeper shadows.

"I find myself lost," she confessed, her words barely disturbing the night air. "I cannot continue this endless flight from what pursues me."

Sebastian reduced the distance between them with measured steps, maintaining steady eye contact. Though the barrier of species prevented him from sharing words she could comprehend, he poured all of his resolution, all of his fierce determination to protect her, into his unwavering gaze.

The wind changed direction with supernatural suddenness, carrying with it an unsettling chill that made the roses tremble in their beds.

The spectre materialised at the garden's furthest reach, its form more substantially defined than ever before, as though it had gained strength from the earlier confrontation. It moved with a terrible, liquid grace that seemed to mock the natural movements of living things, its edges rippling like dark water disturbed by unseen currents.

Elisa became absolutely still, her fingers tightening convulsively around the rose's thorny stem until fresh blood welled between them.

Sebastian issued a sharp warning cry, his wings spreading to their full span as he positioned his small but determined form between Elisa and the approaching horror. The rest of the flock took to the air in a rush of wings and alarmed calls, their dark shapes weaving complex patterns through the trees as they voiced their concerns to one another.

The spectre paused in its advance, its amorphous form seeming to consider Sebastian's defensive stance with an intelligence that was all the more terrifying for its otherness. For a suspended moment that seemed to stretch into eternity, the two faced each other across the moonlit garden – shadow against feathers, darkness against darkness, supernatural force against unwavering will.

Then, with explosive violence, the spectre launched its attack.

Sebastian hurled himself skyward, his talons extended to slash at the spectre's insubstantial form. The contact felt like fighting against smoke given malevolent purpose, each strike meeting a resistance that sent waves of bitter cold through his wings and into his very core. The spectre recoiled from his assault, its form twisting and flickering like a candle flame in a storm as it struck back with whip-like tendrils of living shadow.

Elisa scrambled to regain her footing, still clutching the blood-stained rose as though it might serve as some form of talisman against the darkness. She turned towards the imposing bulk of the manor house, but her steps faltered as the spectre's overwhelming presence pressed against her like a physical weight, attempting to drive her to her knees.

"Run!" Sebastian's cry pierced the night air, his voice rising in desperate urgency even though she couldn't understand his words.

No translation proved necessary. Elisa lurched forward, her bare feet catching and stumbling on the uneven garden path as she abandoned all pretence of grace and fled towards the relative safety of the woods that bordered the estate.

The spectre's attention snapped back to Sebastian with predatory focus, its movements becoming more erratic and dangerous as it pursued him through the moonlit garden. The other members of the flock joined the aerial battle, their combined cries creating a cacophony that echoed through the night as they executed their coordinated attack.

Aurelia streaked past the spectre's writhing form, her sharp beak tearing at its edges with surprising effectiveness. Matthias followed in her wake, his powerful wings generating gusts that seemed to disperse the shadow's substance as he added his own challenge to the chorus. Working in concert, they gradually forced the entity back, driving it towards the deeper shadows that pooled beneath the garden's ancient trees.

Yet even as it retreated, they all knew that it was far from defeated.

***

Elisa finally reached the woodland's edge, her chest heaving as she collapsed against the rough bark of an ancient oak. The rose she had carried throughout her flight slipped from her nerveless fingers, its darkened petals standing in stark relief against the carpet of pale green moss that covered the forest floor.

Sebastian landed beside her with far less than his usual grace, his feathers dishevelled and his wings trembling with deep exhaustion from the confrontation with the spectre.

"You're safe for now," he announced fiercely, though he knew she couldn't hear the words, his gaze fixed on her face, which seemed almost translucent in the filtered moonlight.

Elisa turned to look at him, her expression holding something that transcended mere gratitude or understanding. With painful slowness, she extended one bloodied hand, allowing her fingers to barely brush against the tips of his wing feathers. It marked the first time she had initiated physical contact with him, and the gesture carried a depth of meaning that neither of them could fully articulate nor comprehend.

The spectre continued to lurk at the forest's boundary, manifesting as subtle distortions in the natural darkness. Though it had withdrawn from direct confrontation, its patient malevolence made it clear that it had not abandoned its pursuit.

Sebastian hopped closer to Elisa's huddled form, his dark eyes meeting and holding her gaze with unwavering intensity. She managed to summon a ghost of a smile, though it trembled at the edges like a candle flame in a draft as her hand fell limply back to her lap.

"Thank you," she said breathily, the words barely disturbing the night air. "For whatever you are, whatever this is, thank you."

The flock gathered in the branches overhead, their soft calls to one another carrying notes of uncertainty about what might come next. The night had fallen quiet again, disturbed only by the gentle susurration of leaves in the wind and the gradually steadying rhythm of Elisa's breathing.

Sebastian maintained his protective position at her side, his small but determined form serving as a living barrier between her and the darkness that waited with infinite patience at the edge of the woods. Though he knew the battle was far from over, he silently renewed his vow to stand between her and whatever horrors might emerge from the shadows, for as long as strength remained in his wings.

Chapter Eight

T he first hesitant rays of dawn broke through the tangled canopy of the ancient woods like searching fingers, their fragile warmth gradually pushing back the last stubborn remnants of the long night. Though the air still hung heavy with the burden of recent supernatural violence, the spectre's oppressive presence had finally begun to ebb, retreating like a dark tide into those shadowed places where malevolent things waited and watched with infinite patience.

Elisa remained seated against the massive trunk of an age-old oak, her head resting against its weathered bark as though drawing strength from its centuries of endurance. Her once-pristine wedding gown, now reduced to little more than elegant ruins, bore the stark evidence of her ordeal – dirt ground deeply into the delicate fabric, dried blood creating abstract patterns across the white silk, each stain a testament to her desperate flight through the darkness. Her fingers, still marked by the cruel kiss of rose thorns, lay curled in her lap like wounded birds. Yet there was something different about her in the steel-grey light of early morning, something that hadn't been there before. A certain steadiness had taken root in her bearing, an unwavering quality that suggested the night's terrors had forged something stronger within her rather than breaking her completely.

Sebastian maintained his vigilant position on a low-hanging branch above her head, his dark eyes constantly scanning the surrounding clearing for any hint of threatening movement. He had not abandoned his self-appointed post throughout the entire night, even as the rest of the flock took turns maintaining their protective watch over the fugitive bride. The supernatural battle had extracted its toll from all of them – their wings hung heavy with exhaustion, their usually raucous voices subdued to little more than whispers – but they had succeeded in driving the spectre back into whatever dark realm had spawned it.

For now, at least.

Aurelia descended from the higher branches with careful grace, her sleek feathers catching and reflecting the strengthening morning light like polished obsidian. She alighted beside Sebastian, her bright, intelligent gaze drawn inevitably to Elisa's resting form.

"She possesses more strength than I initially credited her with," Aurelia observed in hushed tones, a note of admiration creeping into her voice.

"Such strength is not a luxury but a necessity," Sebastian replied, his words quiet but carrying an underlying current of iron certainty.

"She cannot remain in this place," Matthias interjected as he joined them from above, his talons gripping the branch with enough force to convey the gravity of his words. "The spectre will inevitably track her down if she lingers anywhere near these cursed grounds."

Sebastian allowed the observation to hang in the air unanswered as he watched Elisa begin to stir, her eyes fluttering open to meet the gentle light that filtered through the forest canopy. She pushed herself into a more upright position with painful slowness, each movement betraying the bone-deep weariness that seemed to inhabit every fibre of her being.

Her gaze drifted around the clearing with growing awareness before finally settling on Sebastian's watchful form.

"You've remained faithful to your vigil," she murmured, her voice roughened by exhaustion.

Sebastian responded by tilting his head slightly, his feathers rustling in a gesture that somehow managed to convey both acknowledgment and reassurance.

A subtle smile touched Elisa's lips, though it carried more sorrow than joy. "When all others have turned away or revealed their true nature, you alone have stood steadfast."

As the morning light strengthened and

expanded, Elisa gradually worked her way to her feet, using the ancient oak's sturdy trunk for support as she fought against waves of dizziness. Her bare feet, scratched and bruised from her desperate flight through the woods, pressed against the cool earth with determined purpose, refusing to acknowledge the pain that each step must have caused. Through gaps in the endless trees, she could just make out the distant silhouette of the manor house, its imposing bulk seeming to loom over the landscape even from this distance.

"There can be no return to that place," she spoke aloud to the morning air, seemingly unaware that her words had an audience more attentive than she realised.

Sebastian responded with a soft, encouraging call as he glided down from his perch to take up position near her feet, his presence offering silent support.

Elisa's gaze dropped to meet his unwavering stare, her brow furrowing with uncertainty. "I find myself without direction," she confessed, her voice wavering between fear and determination. "The path ahead appears as shrouded as the one behind."

The flock began to stir en masse in the branches overhead, their dark forms separating from the shadows as they took to the morning air with purpose. They wheeled above the clearing in ever-widening circles, their calls sharp and clear in the crisp morning air, carrying notes of both urgency and encouragement.

Sebastian joined his brethren in flight, his wings spreading wide as he rose above Elisa's upturned face. His movements were precisely controlled as he banked towards the east, where the ancient woods stretched towards the horizon like an endless green sea.

Elisa tracked his flight with growing understanding, her expression shifting from confusion to dawning comprehension.

"East," she mused softly, her gaze drawn to the brightening horizon as though seeing it with new eyes. She stood motionless for several heartbeats before taking a tentative step in that direction, physically and symbolically moving away from the manor's unpleasant influence.

***

The journey through the dense woodland proved to be an arduous test of endurance. The thick underbrush seemed determined to impede Elisa's progress, thorny vines and low-hanging branches catching at the ruins of her wedding gown as though trying to draw her back. The uneven ground, hidden beneath deceptive carpets of leaves and moss, caused her to stumble repeatedly as she picked her way forward. Yet Sebastian remained a constant presence, his sharp, clear cries serving as both guidance and encouragement when the path ahead seemed unclear or her strength threatened to fail.

The rest of the flock moved in advance of their position, their dark shapes weaving intricate patterns between the ancient trunks as they scouted the safest route forward. Aurelia made frequent returns to check on their progress, her bright eyes watching Elisa with an increasingly complex mixture of curiosity, concern, and growing respect.

"My initial assessment of her strength continues to prove inadequate," Aurelia commented softly as she alighted beside Sebastian during one of Elisa's necessary rest periods.

"Such resilience is not a matter of choice but of survival," Sebastian replied, his tone carrying equal measures of pride and concern.

The dense woodland gradually began to thin as the day progressed, the closely packed trees finally giving way to sun-drenched fields that stretched towards the horizon in endless hues of gold. Elisa came to a halt at the forest's edge, her breath catching audibly in her throat as she gazed out at the unfamiliar expanse that lay before her, full of both promise and uncertainty.

Sebastian took up position on a weathered fence post nearby, his steady gaze never leaving her form as she contemplated this literal and metaphorical threshold.

"This distance should suffice," Matthias declared, his voice carrying a rough note of approval as he settled beside Sebastian. "The spectre's influence won't extend this far, at least not immediately."

Sebastian maintained his silence, watching intently as Elisa gathered her courage and stepped out into the sun-washed field, her movements slow but carrying a new sense of purpose and determination.

***

As the sun climbed steadily towards its zenith, the flock gathered in the spreading branches of a solitary oak that stood sentinel at the field's edge. They maintained their collective vigil as Elisa's figure grew gradually smaller against the vast horizon, the shreds of her white gown catching the light like a distant beacon.

"She'll find her way now," Aurelia declared, her tone carrying a certainty that hadn't been present before.

Matthias offered a low, thoughtful caw as he turned to regard Sebastian with knowing eyes. "You've accomplished what was within your power to do."

Sebastian remained focused on Elisa's diminishing form, his silence speaking volumes about his ongoing concern and commitment.

When she finally vanished from sight,

absorbed into the golden light that bathed the endless fields, Sebastian spread his wings and took to the air with graceful purpose. The rest of the flock followed his lead, their combined voices rising in a chorus that echoed across the open land as they ascended into the endless blue above.

The flock would maintain their protective watch over her, even if their vigil would need to be kept from a greater distance. Such was their sacred duty as guardians of the forgotten, protectors of those souls who found themselves without other allies in their darkest hours. As Sebastian soared through the limitless sky, the warming sun a comfort against his battle-weary feathers, he felt an unshakeable resolve take root in the depths of his being.

Elisa had won her freedom – for the moment, at least.

But should the shadows ever dare to reach for her again, he and his kind would be waiting, ready to rise once more in her defence – for some battles were worth any cost, and some souls were worth protecting until the very end of days.